MAKE YOURSELF AT HOME!

MAKE YOURSELF AT HOME!

SIGNE TORP

CONTENTS

THE BEST BUILDER AWARD

GOES TO...

An igloo in Canada

Crunch, crunch. There's the sound of my father's boots coming to the front door. He dusts the snow off his clothes and settles into the warmth. Even when there's a howling blizzard outside, the inside of our igloo still feels cozy! Our body heat keeps it warm.

I'm Yura and I built this igloo with my family last week. It keeps us safe and warm when we're on long hunting trips. Special skills are needed to build an igloo. An igloo that is built the right way can hold the weight of a person standing on top of it.

AINNGAI!

We built a bed on a raised platform, where it's the warmest. Hot air rises so we sleep as high as we can. To make it even cozier we lined it with animal skins and hung one in front of the door too.

You can make igloos in all different sizes, and connect them to each other using tunnels.

An igloo is a hut made only from snow. The snow is packed into brick-sized chunks and cut with a snow knife. Snow has tiny trapped air pockets, which makes it an excellent insulator. It is a simple and genius construction! The word "igloo" comes from the Inuit word meaning home or shelter. It was developed in Arctic areas where there is a lot of snow and little other building material.

A window can be made using a single block of clear ice.

The only trouble is...needing the bathroom at night! Sometimes it's too cold so we pee inside into a bucket and take it out in the morning.

ENORMOUS FORTRESS

A castle in Germany

A castle is big. It's very, VERY BIG. See how high this one towers next to the trees? The thick stone walls make it dark and cold. Inside, voices boom against the castle walls and echo down the winding corridors.

Castles were built by kings, queens or noble people. They were made for protection. This one uses natural defenses to keep it safe and it was built on a 230-foot-high rock. It's hidden deep in the woods above a river that bends around three of the castle's sides.

Hi I'm Max! My family started building this castle 850 years ago. It took 500 years to finish because it's so huge! We still own it today.

Castles were protected by a drawbridge. Once the drawbridge was raised it was very hard for enemies to break in!

That's our family
shield on the tower.

Only a tiny shaft of light filters
through the many narrow
windows. They are just wide
enough to fire an arrow through
and keep the shooter safe.

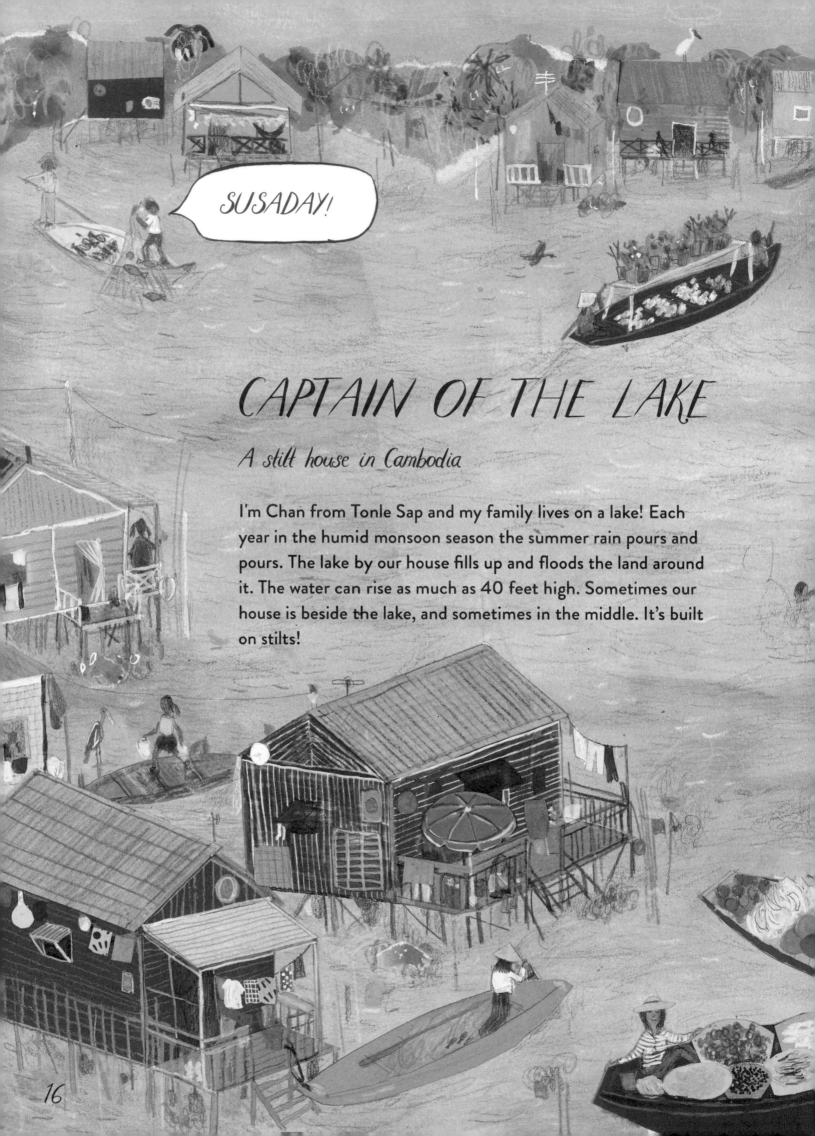

CAPTAIN OF THE LAKE

A stilt house in Cambodia

I'm Chan from Tonle Sap and my family lives on a lake! Each year in the humid monsoon season the summer rain pours and pours. The lake by our house fills up and floods the land around it. The water can rise as much as 40 feet high. Sometimes our house is beside the lake, and sometimes in the middle. It's built on stilts!

When it rains, everything floats. My friends and I know how to row a boat because we paddle our way to school everyday. Come and meet my classmates at the floating school.

The lake is our playground! We jump from boat to boat and play hide-and-seek between the seats of the canoes. At dinner time we paddle home to the captain of the house.

Try some food at the floating market. You can buy anything from fresh fish to bananas and mangoes.

When the lake is high it looks like I am living in a bamboo hut floating on top of the water. From the boat, I can hop straight into my living room!

When the water is low, it's like living in a tree house far above ground. I climb the long bamboo ladder to get to the front door.

There are lots of animals that you won't see anywhere else. Like the spot-billed pelican, which snaps or hisses when it is in its nest.

The Siamese crocodile lurks in the water. Although they're not dangerous, I still keep a close eye out when I'm swimming!

My family are fishermen, like lots of the families living in the Tonle Sap lake. We catch just enough to make a living but not too much. We don't want all the fish to disappear.

TOWER OF COMPUTERS

A skyscraper in New York, U.S.

This skyscraper is 350 feet high, with 30 floors. From the top, the people below look like tiny scurrying dots. Each night, I see the city lights go on. Millions and millions of tiny dots, each one a home in the same city as me. You can't see me but I can see you—I'm Lenny and I live on the 30th floor.

From up here we can see buildings all across the city and Central Park below us. We take our dogs for a walk in the park but it's a long, long way down.

I can count all the buildings I can see just from my bedroom window.

HEY!

With a whole floor to play on, there's plenty of space for a big sleepover.

If it's raining I can go down to the indoor tennis court for games.

"Alexa, can we have some ice cream please?"
"Sorry Lenny and Jada, today is not ice cream day."

We use a smart speaker—"Alexa"—in our house to order groceries and search for the weather forecast. We aren't allowed to ask for Alexa's help at homework time though!

23

SWAYING WITH THE SQUAWKERS

A tree house in Vanuatu

We're Mahana and Lono. Our favorite place to sit is on the balcony of our house at the top of the banyan tree. From here we watch whales blow their watery greetings as we eat breakfast. Bats, parrots and butterflies flicker past. We chatter and sing with the animals, then swing along the branches to get to our treetop bed.

From the treetops we can spy on the land below. We rise at dawn with the sun and sleep when it sets.

Our house is made from all of the things you find nearby. It's simple to build if you know how.

HALO!

Our family eats the food we grow and sells any extra food at the market. We make our own clothes too. Lots of people in this tree house neighborhood swap the things we grow and make, rather than selling them for money.

The banyan tree is a type of fig tree. Its sweet-smelling flowers and fruit attract all sorts of wildlife. We have lots of animal friends...even more when we're eating our dinner. They can be quite pesky when they're hungry.

At a certain time of year, the "hoot hoot" of the animals can sound like a wild orchestra! They don't listen much when we ask them, "Be quiet please, we're trying to sleep."

The banyan tree has aerial roots that spread up and sideways out of the ground. They look like lots of small trunks pushed together, which make the perfect platform to build a house on.

Windmills pump water or grind things like grain, wood or spices. My family and I live in a machine house, it's a home and a workplace.

There are 991 windmills in the Netherlands. A lot of the country is below sea level so the windmills help pump the water away from the lower land.

DANCING HOUSES

A windmill in the Netherlands

What sort of home has sails, moves water, but does not travel? A windmill. The blades that spin are called sails. Frrrt, frrt, frrrt, they clatter past my tiny bedroom window with an almighty racket. I'm Joey by the way and I live in that windmill over there! From afar they look like dancers spinning in the wind, round and round together in time.

The top of the windmill is called the cap. We can rotate it to face the direction of the wind.

In the Netherlands, the position of the sails was once used to pass on messages, such as on special occasions and at sad times. There was also a signal to warn of danger.

When the sails are spinning, the house can shudder and creak.

Our family lives on the first two floors. The further up you go, the smaller the spaces are to live in.

QUIET AND CALM

A siheyuan in Beijing, China

The smell of food wafts through the courtyard. Mother
is cooking for my birthday. There will be a family feast!
Luckily they don't have to come far. Everyone lives together
in my home—my grandparents, parents, my brother and me.
I'm Liu and I live in a siheyuan house.

The courtyard is full of plants. I help my granny feed the animals and water the plants after school.

The entrance gate is at the southeast corner. It's painted bright red for luck and has a dragon door knocker. Outside the gate there are stone lions for protection.

The different parts of the buildings are for different members of my family. My grandparents live in one wing, my parents in another, and my brother and I have our own wing.

31

It's my job to open the locks. A lock is like an elevator for boats. The water gushes in and the boat sinks down. Sometimes it's the other way and we move up. Off we go again, bobbing to a new place!

Hi, I'm Sofia, and my home can float through hills, across valleys, under roads and railways or on big aqueducts.

HELLO!

We share the water with ducks and swans, and if you're lucky you might spot a kingfisher! At night foxes dash along the towpaths, too.

BOBBING BEDS

A narrowboat in London, U.K.

This boat isn't made to cross the big oceans, it's made to chug along thin canals in the UK. The boats can be up to 6 feet wide and 72 feet long. It's tight inside, so you have only the things you need. No more, no less.

We named our boat Amethyst and it is home to me,
my parents and two cats! It's decorated with roses,
which I helped to paint.

We move along the canals and make new friends wherever we go. When we stop in one place, our narrowboats make friendly floating neighborhoods.

It can be busy along the waterways. People who watch or wave as we pass by are called "gongoozlers." They like to look as we open the locks and move along the canal.

COOL AS A CUCUMBER

Cave houses in Tunisia

It's not easy to stay cool when you live near the Sahara, which is one of the hottest deserts in the world. Unless you build an underground house.

Humans have lived in different kinds of caves for a very long time. Some have been in use for 700 years.

The doors and windows lead into the caves. We tunnel along to carve out chambers and passageways. They connect like a maze, or a rabbit's warren.

SALAM!

"Near the great hill, to the right of the palm tree,"—that's how to get to my house. Friends sometimes get lost. It's hard to see our house from afar.

The passageways are big enough for people to walk through without having to bend down.

I am Samira and my home was made by digging a deep hole in the ground. The space in the middle is the courtyard.

Underground villages like mine were unknown to most of the world until they were made famous by the film *Star Wars*.

Our cave homes stay warm during the freezing desert nights. The temperature inside remains the same during the day and night.

MOVING ACROSS MOUNTAINS

A ger in Mongolia

Does your home fit on the back of a yak? Can it travel across mountains and be packed up in a day? Mine does! I'm Alma and my home is called a ger. Gers have been used for 3,000 years by cattle herders in Mongolia.

My family and I are nomads. We own yaks and goats, which we shuffle across the valleys to find fresh grass. Our house needs to be quick and easy to put up.

When it's very rainy, we dig a trench around the ger to collect water. It's a bit like a castle's moat.

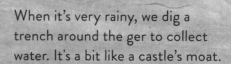

The mountain passes have ferocious winds that whip cold and strong against the canvas sides. The round shape of our ger is made to be sturdy against it.

Here by the chimney is the crown of our ger. It's decorated with wood, reeds and fabrics. It was made by my grandmother and has been passed down the generations.

Lots of gers have up to five layers of animal wool, which are covered by canvas. They are usually 6.5 feet high.

This ger took an hour to set up (some take three).

My favorite spot is in the middle, right next to the warm stove...but it does get a bit smoky by the fire.

Our door always faces south, away from the northern wind.

43

GLOSSARY

Aerial roots   Roots that grow aboveground rather than below.

Aqueduct   A large structure built to carry plenty of water across land.

Arctic   An extremely cold area around the North Pole.

Banyan tree   A big fig tree whose branches send out roots to the ground.

Canopy bed   A bed with a piece of cloth across the top to form a roof.

Gongoozler   Someone who watches canal life but doesn't take part.

Insulator   Material that stops warmth from escaping. A house might be built with insulation to keep heat in.

Locks (canal)   Locks are gateways built into a canal to raise and lower the level of water. They help boats move across uneven land.

Monsoon   A tropical rainy season that happens in parts of Asia.

Narrowboat   A small barge that travels on canals.

Nomad   People who move from place to place and do not live in a fixed location.

Sahara   The world's largest hot desert.

Species   A group of animals, plants or living things that share important characteristics.

Towpath   A path beside a river or canal, used in the past by horses pulling boats.

Yak   A type of large cattle that has horns and long hair.

INDEX

For my parents Tuppi and Svenning.
Thank you for being so great at making homes!

Make Yourself at Home © 2020 Thames & Hudson Ltd, London
Text and illustrations © 2020 Signe Torp

Copyedited by AHA editorial
Designed by Barbara Ward

First published in 2020 in the United States of America by
Thames & Hudson Inc., 500 Fifth Avenue, New York, New York 10110

Library of Congress Control Number 2020931415

ISBN 978-0-500-65214-5

Printed and bound in China by RR Donnelley

Be the first to know about our new releases,
exclusive content and author events by visiting
thamesandhudson.com
thamesandhudsonusa.com
thamesandhudson.com.au